a cat's fantasy

Queen Of Sofa Mountain

written & illustrated

by

Brent Warren

imagelust / studios

for

jesse and shirley ujest

PUBLISHED BY IMAGELUST STUDIOS
P.O. BOX 938 -NEDERLAND, CO. 80466
printed in USA

Library of Congress Catalog Card Number
93-77890

ISBN   1-883350-01-8 (paperback)

3 5 7 10 8 6 4 2

THE CAT SAT

looking out across the vast flat "carpet tundra" plateau.

N the distance, on the other side, barely visible through the room dusk haze,

A Magnificent Mountain Stood !

Huge it was, in all dimensions, towering tall, looming wide over all the living room country, dwarfing the armchair hills and stool buttes with its monstrous mountain mass.

From the West, air-conditioned winds swept through, over the bloom and pasture, caressing each mountain contour with air fingers. Circulating, the winds absorbed a variety of scented essences into cloud pockets, mingled but for a moment or two, and then, flowed, out across the tundra plateau, carrying the booty wisps of enticement to the nose and soul of one inquisitive cat.

the cat's name was Shirley
(a modern translation meaning "Quest Seeker")

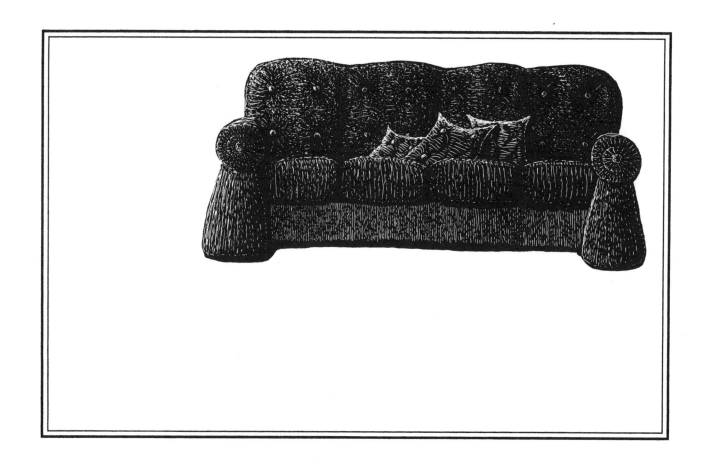

the mountain was called Sofa.
(An ancient feline word meaning, "Large sit challenge object")

There was treasure on top of Sofa mountain!
What better quest could there possibly be - than the quest for treasure.

Anticipation awoke, and Shirley," the cat of determination" prepared for exploration.
Endurance, strength, and of course, curiosity, ushered forth invitations to all instincts:
"Unite Now!" "Climb Sofa mountain!" "Find the great treasure!"

From just inside the right ear, an eccentric conscience of enthusiasm shouted out assurances for instant action, "You can do it! Go Forth Cat!"
At the same time, with studied debate, the conservative left ear conscience issued warnings to the feline brain, "Don't go! Stay put! There are many dangers out there!"

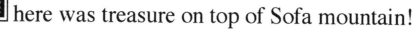

The mountain beyond created a pastel peace upon the eyes. Standing quiet and serene, its textured beauty offered an invisible hand of love and trust - or so it seemed.

THE old ones taught that perils a plenty lurk amongst silent shadows in the day by day ritual of cat survival.

Stick pin bushes, Silverware logs, Magazine ice, Sliding drawer teeth, Tidal sink basins, Bathtub oceans, Toilet whirlpools, Stovetop fire geysers, Venus mouse traps, Bookshelf land-slides, Rocking chair tail crushers - to name a few - dormant in veiled corners, awaiting the precise moment to pounce with unexpected catastrophe.

One careless step meant falling prey to disaster.

Shirley stared across the in-between with worry on her face.

This slumberesque mountain was no exception.

Upon its delicate pathways were many sinister dangers.

And topping the list were the GIANTS.

Intelligent life forms with immeasurable powers, GIANTS ruled the land.

They made laws and enforced them with swift retaliation--- yet they also gave food and water in kindness, and, alas, it was the GIANTS who held the key to the treasure of Sofa Mountain.

Shirley with all her cat wisdom and cat logic had tried to understand the GIANTS in their unpredictable complexity, but gave up, content with the simple ability to read their mood at the moment of encounter.

"Go find the treasure," enticed the right ear conscience!

Pondering the problems, the feline trailblazer rose to her feet and responded, "No problem."

Thus the expedition began.

A "Sacajawea" with whiskers set out across the carpet tundra.

The ground was soft. Carpet grass kept footsteps quiet. Darkness and shadow surrounded on all sides. Shirley dared not to slow her gait. Out there, possibly anywhere, were seductions and distractions, famous for their ability to tantalize the feline weakness for frolic and play.

With head held high and eyes fixed straight ahead, Shirley walked a steady path around the "cardboard box cave", through the "wool ball bushes", over the "paper wad rocks". Even a fat juicy mouse escaped her consideration.

"Don't you want to stop and play just a wee bit?" inquired the left ear.

"NO!" said the right.

Suddenly, an aroma, pungent and sweet, filled the air. Shirley broke stride, stopped and turned her nose. There, within paw's reach, was a pile of catnip-filled play toys and small critter replicas. They begged investigation.

A cat of little integrity would have taken this bait, leaving all thoughts of mountain and treasure behind. Luckily, a strong will of self denial prevailed.

The cat of determination filled her senses with visions of adventure - and walked on.

"Good girl!" rejoiced the right ear.

he confluence between flat and tall.

The journey across the plateau seemed like a cats eternity, weaving past rocker ravine, and wastebasket wash, and garment gully, ending, uneventfully, at last, with cat nostrils pressed against a cloth cliff. The very base of the mountain.

From here on the geography ascended vertically. Shirley tilted her head back as far as it would go, trying to see some hint of destination. There was none, only the lofting spectacle of vermilion velvet rock. This was the first obstacle, the "great wall".

ASTOUNDING!

Mild fear lumped in her throat. Shirley established base camp, a place to rest and gather courage.

Curling into traditional ball shape slumber position, the adventurer catnapped. Subconscious thoughts planned expedition routes. Vivid dreams kept glimpses of treasure alive, while outside, in the real world, tranquil sleep vibrations swam with the rainbow shadows and became one with the mountain called Sofa!

sudden dawn woke the cat. The incandescent sunrise!

Semiconscious, Shirley peeked out through eye slits into the glare of morning. Gradually the images before her became sharp and distinct. Illumination made the spectacle of the mountain all the more awesome.

An abrupt thought crossed her mind. A GIANT must be near! They and they alone created the sunrises and sunsets incandescent. A good sign!

A decision! To go forth, or to turn back?

Time was now a valued commodity. The left and right ears continued their debate. From deep within the cliff walls there came music, faint, yet definite songs, filling the outside air with expansion and compression lyrics. Spring steel, wood, and foam rubber formed chorus and chanted a mesmerizing verse.

'twas the soul of the mountain singing, "Who will climb me?"

Shirley, the cat of determination, replied, "I will!"

Claws! (klos) *1. Fantastic, irreplaceable, all purpose tools of the feline trade. 2. Retractable talons of razor sharpness, hidden in peaceful storage until instant duty calls them forth.*

Ten built-in can openers were exposed to the elements, where-upon a sharpening ritual was performed. With syncopated movements, one forepaw and then the other stroked downward, dragging the hook knives against the great wall surface, over and over and over again, until each needle point sparkled.

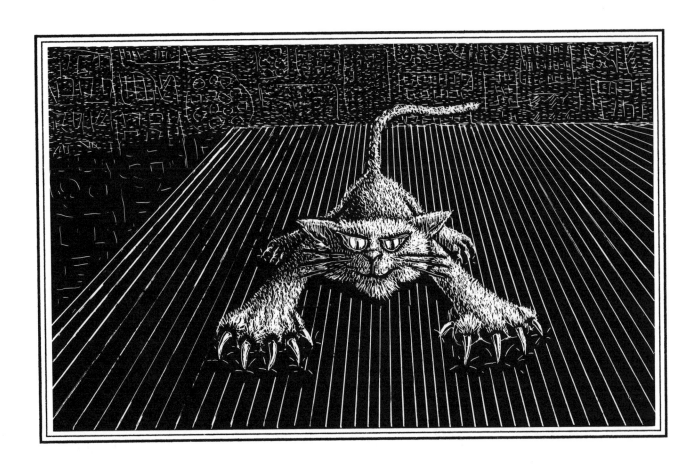

Shirley sat back on her rear legs and looked up. "Lets do it!"

"Hubba,Hubba,Hubba!" rejoiced the right ear.

A countdown began, " Nine- eight- seven," eyes locked on a target.

"Six- five- four," last minute check with systems go.

"Three- two- one," all body strengths gathered into spring-like tension. "ZERO!"

They released, and with a strong skyward jump, Shirley flew toward a quest.

A dig in landing was made a thousand cat feet off the ground.

This was not the best of places to tarry, dangling from the side of the great wall like moss on a tree. A forbidden zone it was.

"No climbing mountain walls and cliffs!"

This was _number one law_ from the world of GIANTS and capture in this vulnerable position meant a sharp sting on the rear end from an attacking magazine log. Instant pain and fear, skillfully designed by the GIANTS to launch any dangling cat into a frantic uncontrolled run for sanctuary.

"Let's move it," shouted both ears.

The cat agreed !

A push, a pull, another push, one paw after the other gripped and released. Adrenalin awoke, inertia gave way to momentum. Slowly, Shirley's body began to inch upwards along the cliff face. Pull, grunt, lift! Her gaze locked in but one direction. Heave to! Ascending, slowly, steadily. Strain, thrust, grip! Muscles throbbing with pain messages. The wall rose forever.

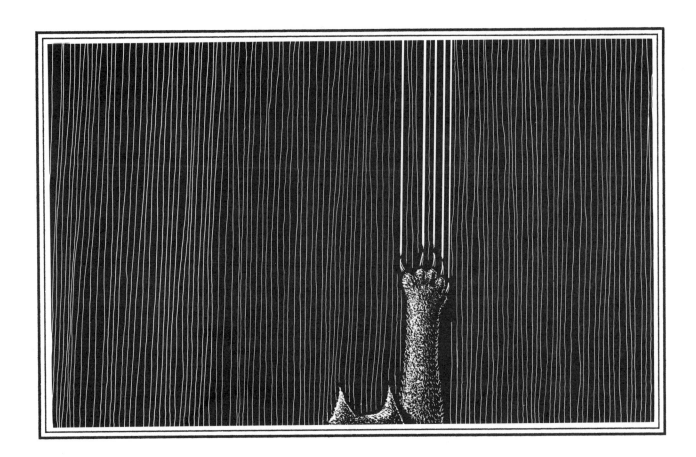

paw slipped.

Shirley fell.

The wall rushed by in front of her. So did memories from her previous two lives.

Blindly grabbing with all strengths she caught hold, stopping the plummet.

Shaken, confused, yet without contrary thought, she began again, hoisting toward the ceiling sky. Ugh, agh, ech! Cat hours, year minutes dragged by.

There!

A vision of wonder appeared. The arm cornice came into view, then within reach. Shirley tried to smile but her tongue was in the way.

"Up and over," coached the right ear.

Hind paws were raised parallel with the side of her head. They gripped deep into the velvet rock. Shirley took a deep breath- and let go.

Front legs shot out. Rear legs pushed. A whirl of moving air!

The entire cat lung capacity expelled itself forcibly into the atmosphere.

Wooooof, meow, pooof, purrrr, THUD!

AT eyes slowly opened.

A new world appeared to the creature who now lounged spread eagle along the narrow ledge of the sofa arm cornice.

Vermilion velvet topsoil cascaded across the concave and convex. Here and there gentle thread flowers grew in petrified stances. Rock shadows painted majestic shapes upon the decor canvas in an effort to hide, to no avail, the wear and tear erosion scars, compliments of the domicile seasons from years bygone.

It looked extremely wonderful and felt very solid.

"I have to admit your climb was nicely done!" exclaimed the left ear.

"Ditto!" from the right.

In first hurtle triumph, air was sucked in to reward her body. A meow of delight frothed forth. Shirley peeked cautiously down the face of the great wall. She could see the far below, far behind her.

A flash out of the corner of her eye demanded attention. High above, surrounded by lampshade clouds, the pear shaped incandescent sun gave off brilliant light. It was perched on the tip top of a thin pillar which lifted gracefully, with art deco flamboyance, up from the tundra floor. This spectacle of illumination pulled Shirley to her feet.

The adventurer's curiosity to find out "what's just beyond, round the corner, over that hill" began to grow inside her psyche.

The brief intermission ended. A journey forward along the rounded terrain began with slow, carefully placed steps. The pleated fabric soil tickled the bottom of her paws.

Shirley was on the verge of a giggle when an apparition appeared —-

and stopped her short in her tracks.

COMING straight at her was another cat. Instantly claws sprang forth. Neck fur stood to attention. A low hissing growl emerged as a warning to this feline stranger. Shirley had no intention of retreat.

In preparation for battle, Shirley hunched her back as tall as she could. The stranger cat took a similar stance. Shirley opened her mouth wide to show fangs, so did the stranger.

Negotiations were over! There was now only one course of action. Shirley threw her claws directly at the face of the intruder. Instantly, the stranger did the same back toward Shirley. Their paws, bent for destruction, met. Wham-whack-crunch! It was as if a brick wall had materialized between the two opponents. The claw weapons crashed abruptly against a field of solid matter. The expected target of flesh and fur was missing. A bewildered cat doubled over from the sting of pain.

Licking a throbbing paw, the wounded conqueror began to survey this "right of passage" competitor.

The stranger sat across the way and appeared to be doing the same.

An in-depth study of face, shoulders, fur color, body size filled the idle moments. This stranger, suddenly, looked very familiar. A glint of recognition!

"Wait a minute," thought Shirley, staring straight into the stare back eyes of the rival before her,   "That cat looks a lot like — —ME!"

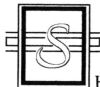

HIRLEY made every move in her repertoire.

A wiggle, a shake, a shimmy, as well as an unrehearsed dance of ears, eyes, nose, and tail. Low and behold, the stranger cat did the exact same moves at the exact same time.   It became perfectly clear. "Genghis Shirley" had just done battle with herself, or a reflection of herself that is. Coming into focus, was a tall, smooth, cylindrical, very solid, clear ice structure, half full of water. A "glass pond."

Shirley fell forward, hugging the sides of the sleek crystal structure. Laughing at the top of her meow, laughing until her sides hurt. "A glass pond," she chuckled as she kissed the clear cool container, " how silly of me not to see it."

"A GLASS POND!"

A loud thought.

The laughter stopped. This was no laughing matter. She took a big gulp and let go of the trembling cylindroid, stepping back very carefully.

The Giants were very protective of these glass ponds.

GIANT law number two: **"Don't mess with glass ponds!"**

They could tip and spill and fall and break into a million pieces, very easily, at the slightest touch.

It was a miracle that the full force impact did not send the glass pond on a disastrous journey to the tundra floor below. Luckily it still stood in one piece.

Left ear stuck in its two bits, "Better go back while you can!"
Right ear, to the defense, "You've come too far to go back!"
"Let's get out of here!" commanded the cat explorer.

Using feline agility a fur covered body managed to squeeze between glass pond and ledge edge without a single movement from the fragile reservoir.   "Whew!"

With head held pride high, Shirley continued forward. She did not look back, nor did she look down.

Had she done so, the newspaper glacier would have been seen in time.

THERE is an expression which may appear on a cat's face, indicating that it, the cat, has realized too late, that it may have stepped into or onto something that it should not have stepped into or onto - and is too afraid to look down, knowing that if it does look down and verify beyond a reason of a doubt that some big bad no-no has indeed been stepped into or onto - then most definitely a full mega-force message will be broadcast from the cat brain with but one word,

stupid !

This was the expression on Shirley's face.

OO Late!

Shirley was smack-dab in the middle of the "newspaper glacier". All around her a crumpled collection of white paper pages drooped and sprawled in a careless cast-off repose. Printed black and white letters, designs and photographs (mostly of Giants) stared up from the sheets.

Early detection might have meant a chance for escape - a leap over, a jump around. Alas, one brief second of self-adulation had been diverted into the core of a very tricky situation.

Choices were two: Shirley could stand there, not moving, a solidified cat, for days, maybe weeks, until rescue came.

Or, she could attempt a step by step retreat off the glacier, praying that it held together.

The latter choice was chosen.

"Good luck," said the left ear.

"Good luck," said the right.

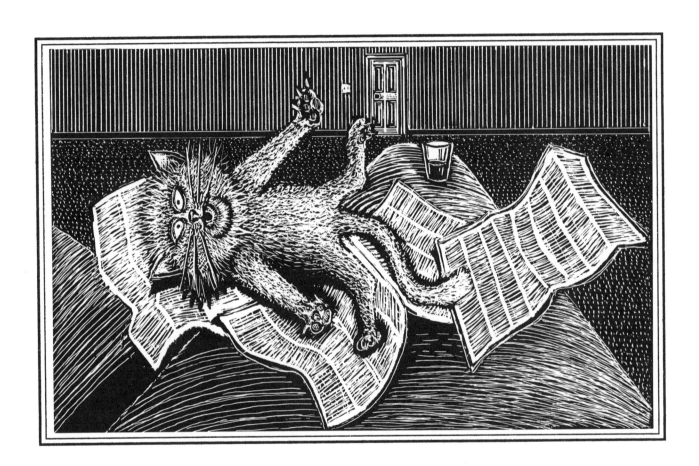

ONE cautious foot crept procrastinatingly forward and then the other. The paper crinkled with each movement. Shirley cringed with each crinkle.

It happened just as a hind foot lifted. The precarious ground under foot suddenly became liquid in motion. The crisp crinkle sound fell into a "Swoooosh". Paper began to slide in all directions. A loud meow of panic bellowed forth in a cat's translation of "AVALANCHE!"

Claws found only layer upon layer of cascading paper to cling onto. Shirley closed her eyes and tried to hold on. A split second later a frazzled, dumbfounded cat was flung out into the mid air of nothing, falling into the clutches of fate.

"Eeeeeooooooohhhhhhhh!"

The arm cornice was bare and silent. The glacier was gone —-

and so was Shirley.

$\mathcal{L}$uck was in the wind.

Saved from a plunge down the great wall, the "newspaper avalanche" took Shirley on the opposite, easterly course, into the valley of pillow rocks.

It left the feline body doubled in half, wedged upside down in a shadowed corner.

The "cat of determination" looked more like a used furry appliance in discard than a great climber of mountains.

Images of the Giants, treasure, and mother shocked Shirley back to her senses. Instinct began a wiggling, jiggling, twisting wave of body motion followed by a beautifully performed roll out maneuver.

This did the trick, lifting the compressed conqueror into the proper status of stance righted.

A quick survey of surroundings was taken.

The newly formed avalanche snow paper fields offered bright white contrast to the soft red of the velvet countryside.

Ripples of low rolling cushion hills flowed toward the horizon. On one side, a drop off overlooked the vastness of the living room country. On the other side, hulks of floral covered pillow rocks delicately balanced upon one another. Behind these rocks, in a long vertical formation, the ascending mass of another impressive cliff barricade towered toward the incandescent sun.   Shirley knew!

This was the route to the summit of the mountain.

Without taking her eyes from the heavens above, one single step forward,

"FLASH, POOF" — — —!

As if a magician's wand had waved and provided abracadabra,

Shirley vanished from everywhere.

However, somewhere out there in the cushioned terra firma, a faint muffled "meow" rose and drifted

a muted hint to the existence of unseen life.

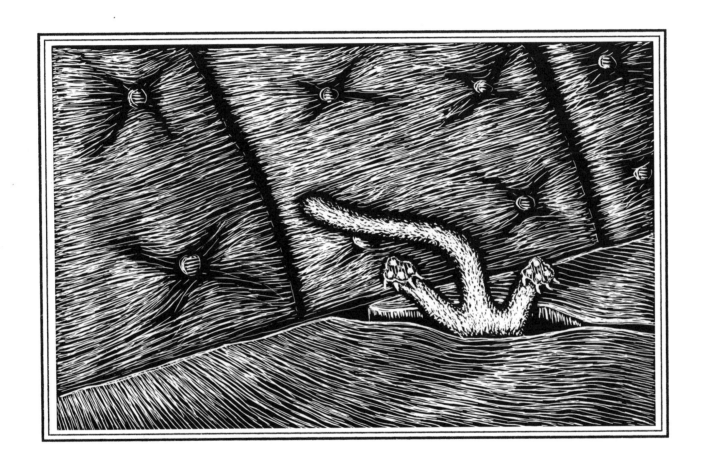

I T is common sense to think that an explorer who had just gone through two harrowing near-misses with tragedy would have been on peak guard against mistake. The price of carelessness without question could cost the victim dignity, the loss of a goal and in some cases the essence of life itself.

Why Shirley had again forgotten to look down as she walked was beyond speculation.

A plunge, headfirst, into a "cushion canyon crevasse" was the consequence.

Amongst the vegetation of the valley, one piece of foliage stood out. A thin snake like furry thing swaying back and forth. It was the tail of a cat, the last remaining tip of feline iceberg visible above ground. The rest was being sucked into the suffocating crevasse. For Shirley, there was now only darkness in a silent void where breathing became thick labor. As she slowly sank deeper and deeper, the walls closed tighter and tighter.

The constrictor and its prey!

"Am I to become but a paper thin semblance of myself," a crushing thought from a creature now reduced to a bookmark between the pages of a landscape.

'Twas not a pleasant position for a lady to be in.

A feline obituary rolled across the brain cells of the trapped. It read;

"years of searching for a missing climber cat found success today when a skeleton was discovered way down in one of those cushion canyons crevasses up on sofa mountain. The remains have been unquestionably identified as that of Shirley, the cat of determination."

SHIRLEY could do little more than stick out her tongue, blink her eyelids, and flex her toes. With every attempt to escape, exhaustion flooded in, and the cushion walls closed the narrow gap by yet another unforgiving measure.

Shirley's head touched bottom. Her tongue felt something cold and metallic, flat, yet circular with raised texture. A coin!

She licked again and this time felt an earring on the left, and then a button to the right.

An awesome world began to appear, illuminated by a ghostly phosphorescent glow. Faint shapes were sprawled about in every direction. A collectorium of abundant junk. A mouth fell open in amazement.

She knew where she must be - the "burial ground of lost objects".

"Beware the "cushion canyons crevasses" where one of this and one of that, coins and cards, rings and things, thimbles and tacks - and unwary cats, get swallowed into voids of black." The warning words of her ancestors!

These stories had been told to her grandfathers by their grandfathers, and their grandfathers before them.

Very old stories they were.

One fable was of a dark land where possessions of the Giants got lost forever. It was a frightening story, taken only to be the product of vivid imaginations.

But now, Shirley saw truth.

Taking a somber position amongst the writing implements, broaches, jewelry, bits of food, shards of clothing, and other trivial, brick-a-brack - she was, in fact, a new resident in this ghastly place of legend-destined to lie extinct in the abyss of the cushion canyon forever.

"I told you to go back," retorted the left ear. It might have been right," admitted the right ear.

"This is the end!" thought sardine imitator Shirley.

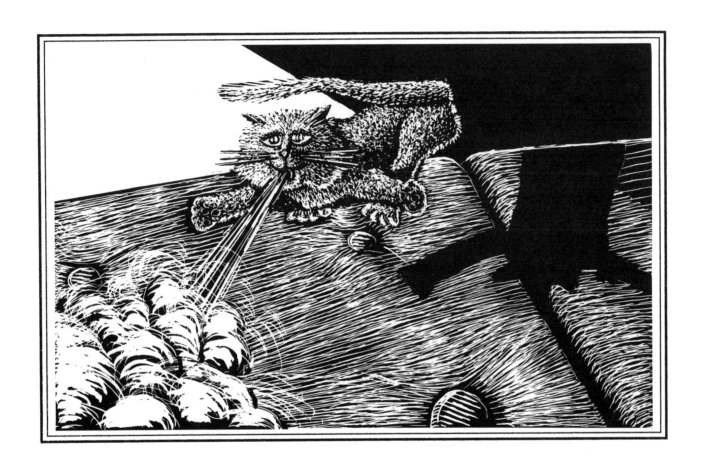

IR, as well as the ability to breathe it, was becoming a rare commodity. "What's this?"

A food smell set Shirley's nose to twitching. Cheese, tomato, flour, pepperoni, and hummmm, spices of many kinds, blended together into one great big lump of familiar aroma.

"PIZZA!" An Italian tidbit refugee from the menu of some GIANTS dinner."

The fragrance caused Shirley's mouth to salivate with hunger. However, the interior of her nose initiated a completely different response - instant allergic reaction.

Basil, oregano, tarragon, sage, thyme, and especially garlic, merged into one huge aromatic feather which headed straight for the tickle zone. Shirley's nose began to spasm, to the left, to the right, up, down, back and forth. Pressure built quickly inside. A sneeze was forming. Instinct made her try to hold it in.

Cheeks were bulging, eyes were popping, an explosion was imminent.

Fleas abandoned the fur ship and jumped to safety .

For one eternal second there was stark silence.

Then, in stereo, a tremendous "achooooooooo" shattered the tranquil mountainscape surface. Echoes rebounded against every cliff.

A bombastic sneeze shook the underground. The cushion canyon silo let go!

A missile-cat shot up and away, streaking through the air, arcing a parabolic trajectory back toward sofa earth.   She was free!

APLOP!

The impact dust settled. The haze parted. A frazzled mass of cat appeared, deposited back in the same valley corner where not so long ago a similar pose of inversion had been struck. She wore freedom like a smile.

"Light, wonderful light, blinding light, white light, opposite of blackness light," rejoiced Shirley, "Light with rainbows and auras and density." How beautifully it filled her eyes.

Blurred visions of catnip juleps, desert isles, and 2% milk beaches with bikini-clad mice entertained her fantasies as recovery from the great rocket sneeze took affect.

Shirley performed another "roll out" maneuver to achieve uprightness.

"Welcome back!" shouted both ears in unison.

"Something is trying to tell me something!" was her perplexed thought.

One mishap after another is enough to make the strongest cat turn tail and run. Shirley was considering this very notion when "cat conscience, right ear faction" took the podium, "The treasure! You're very near! You've come so far! Don't give up!"

Over and over these words circled through the pandemonium of the after-sneeze.

With body shaken but spirit undamaged, Shirley stood and let echo a loud meow: cat slang meaning, "Go for it!"

Dropping back onto her haunches, she once again prepared for flight.

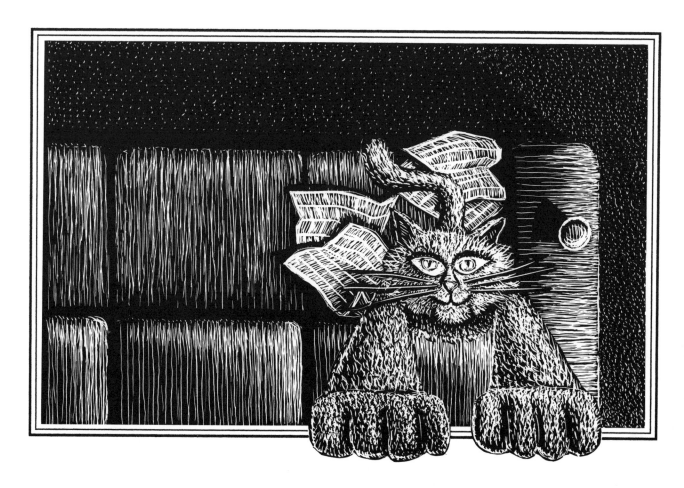

A powerful surge of raw muscle energy supplied the lifting take-off.

THIS was a leap made in mythology, more bird than cat-like.

Shirley, the feline flyer, spread footwings and soared into the upper atmospheres. She was one with air, diving through stars and planets, free-falling with comets, conversing with all the heavens, until gravity, alas, began its downward pull.

With Olympian grace, the silky aerodynamic body floated inbound toward terra sofa, making a smooth, four-footed landing upon the topmost stratospheric ledge, the summit of sofa mountain!

That uncontrollable inner emotion known as "purr" spewed forth and set her heart racing with jubilation.

Time to sit and breathe in the wonderfulness of all wonderful things.

A moments moment to look and rejoice in all directions.

It was the top of the world!

Illumination streaked into the lower corners of everywhere, giving sneak previews of texture features far below on the carpet tundra floor. Elongated shadows of familiar objects stretched out to where the sun's rays could not reach.

Shirley photographed it all with her eyes, missing not a single performance by the players of light.

he incandescent sun was very close.

Above the cloudshade, a perfectly formed circle of light floated in space, the incandescent moon.

Behind and above, wallpaper sky came to a linear end as it joined with the ceiling heaven to form cosmos. Colorful sky flowers faded into gray, gray melted to black, and black in turn allowed all the bright dazzling star specks to appear.

Shirley would have sat there forever, but she sniffed the air. An air finger of fragrant identification was unmistakable.

A GIANT was near!

Her ears started scouting for GIANT sounds. Talking, laughing, coughing, belching, snoring, any sound would do, except snoring, which meant that GIANTS were in no condition to dispense treasures.

There! A tender humming reverberation coming from the East.

Shirley jumped to her feet and began a fast walk along the top ledge, being very, very careful to look down as she stepped.   'Twas no time to blow it!

𝕿HE summit ledge finale.

The feline explorer approached silently. Hanging off the front side of the cliff wall appeared to be an enormous bush. Curiosity pulled her closer for an examination of this peculiar outgrowth, praying that it just might offer a resolve to her quest.

"HOORAY!" The bush moved. Shirley saw what she hoped to see.

A face was attached to the bush, the face of a GIANT.

Shirley's excitement was hard to contain. She jumped up and down, clapping her paws together in celebration of victory.

Had she a flag it would be unfurled and hoisted high as in loud voice the world informed "I, Shirley, hereby claim the treasure of Sofa Mountain in the name of all felines great and small!"

One thing was left to do- claim the treasure!

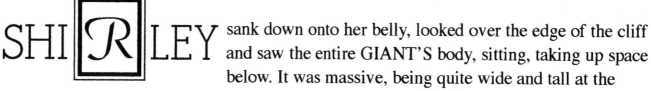SHI R LEY sank down onto her belly, looked over the edge of the cliff and saw the entire GIANT'S body, sitting, taking up space below. It was massive, being quite wide and tall at the same time. Way, way down on the tundra plateau floor, a pair of slipper covered feet could be made out. From there upwards, a comfortable looking fuzzy fabric environment curved and tucked and generally covered the rest of the form.

In the air, the lovely homing perfume took control of the olfactory.

It was a female GIANT. She took no notice of the mountain climbing cat which lounged next to her. She seemed in a trance, looking steadily down into her lap where a stack of white paper rested between her fingers.

"It's now or never!" Shirley let out a mellow "meow."

The GIANT looked up from her lap and peeked over her shoulder, smiled, and spoke, "Why, hello Shirley, where did you come from?"

Shirley spoke back, "Meow, meow, meow, meow, meow, meow, meow, meow!" This explained all to the GIANT, the complete story of the long, strenuous journey up from the carpet plateau floor. The "near fatal" encounters with, and escapes from the ambushes along the way. The joy of being here on top of sofa mountain.

In a humble tone the cat explorer asked ever so politely if a treasure might be collected. The GIANT seemed to understand, slipping a giant hand gently under Shirley's belly, raising her with incredible ease from the ledge perch, and lowering a totally relaxed and trusting cat body into the furry tranquillity of a giant lap.

GIANT hands encircled a soft lump of bliss, once a cat's head.

Giant fingers began undulating massage upon the ears, neck, forehead, cheeks, chin, and all areas in-between. From nose to tail and back again, many times, they stroked and caressed.

Shirley was lost to ecstasy.

Quivering, quavering, shivering with delight, a wide ear to ear grin gave assurances that Nirvana had been reached.

This then was the great cat treasure.

The grand reward!

Shirley- explorer, curious adventurer, death-defying mountain climber extordinaire, had earned it well.

The hands stopped and moved away, revealing on top of Shirley's head, a small patch of fur standing straight up in a ragged circle.

It looked like a little crown.

The symbolic treasure suddenly evolved into a ceremonial pageant complimenting the proceedings of a great coronation.

"HEAR YE, HEAR YE, Shirley, 'the cat of determination' is duly proclaimed royalty; THE QUEEN OF SOFA MOUNTAIN."

As she rode the sandhorse of contented dreams into the land of peaceful slumber, Shirley contemplated all the risks against all the rewards of sofa mountain.
Would she again seek its challenge?
Within, a conjecture germinated:

Surely Shirley, as she has done today, and the day before that, and the day before that, and the day before, for as long as time could remember, would indeed, attempt this climb again — tomorrow!

The Images in this book were created using scratchboard. Scratchboard is a white chalk covered board which is then inked black. Images are made by scratching white lines into the black by using sharp needle like implements.

This book was produced with environmental concern
Using only RECYCLED PAPER and SOYBEAN INKS